The Best-Dressed BEAR

Scholastic Children's Books,
Commonwealth House, 1 – 19 New Oxford Street,
London WC1A 1NU, UK
a division of Scholastic Ltd
London ~ New York ~ Toronto ~ Sydney ~ Auckland
Mexico City ~ New Delhi ~ Hong Kong

First published in New Zealand by Scholastic New Zealand Ltd, 2002
This paperback edition first published in the UK by Scholastic Ltd, 2002

Text copyright © Diana Noonan, 2002
Illustrations copyright © Elizabeth Fuller, 2002

ISBN 0 439 98274 X

Printed in Italy by Amadeus S. p. A. - Rome

2 4 6 8 10 9 7 5 3 1

The rights of Diana Noonan and Elizabeth Fuller to be identified as the
author and illustrator of this work respectively have been asserted by them in
accordance with the Copyright, Designs and Patents Act, 1988.

THE
Best-Dressed
BEAR

Diana Noonan

Illustrated by Elizabeth Fuller

It was past bedtime.
Tim was supposed to be asleep
but he felt strange inside.

He sucked Toby's left ear hard.
He couldn't stop thinking about
the clothes that Mum had sorted out
that afternoon.

She was going to give them all away
to the charity shop.

Tim squeezed Toby tight.
Then he sat up in bed.

The give-away clothes were in the
hall cupboard in a big plastic bag.
Tim towed the bag back to his room.
He hoped Mum wouldn't hear it rustle.

Inside the bag, Tim found
his old playschool jersey
that Dad had knitted.
It had lots of different-
coloured stripes in it.

He and Dad had counted
them one day at the park.
It had duck buttons on the neck.

He found his last year's
Christmas-present shorts from Gran.

He found the teddy slippers that Toby
had given him for his third birthday.
He wished he could still fit them.

Tim took a shaky breath.

He pulled the stripy
playschool jersey
over his head.

He tugged and tugged
until his head popped out
through the neck hole.

He pushed his arms hard
into the sleeves.

Tim felt really
squashed up inside
the jersey – and he
felt really squashed
up inside himself.

Suddenly, his bottom
lip went wobbly.

He hugged Toby tight,
but his eyes still
went watery.

"Oh dear,"
said a voice.

It was Mum.

Tim tried to pull the jersey off
but he was stuck inside it.
He felt hot and sticky.

"What's wrong?" Mum asked.

"I don't want to get bigger," said Tim.
"I want to stay the same."

Mum helped Tim out of the jersey.

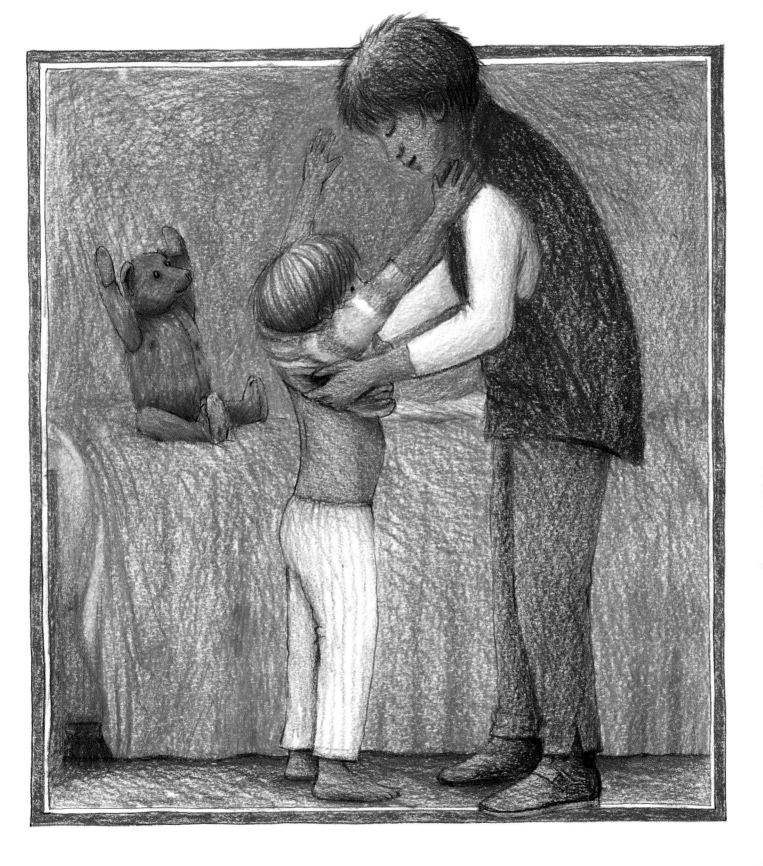

Then she gave him a big cuddle.

"I know just what you mean," she said.
"But there are lots of fun things
about being bigger, too.
You can walk to the shop by yourself.
You can make popcorn in the microwave.
You can ride your two-wheeler."

Tim felt a bit better when Mum said that.
But he still wished he could keep his stripy jersey.

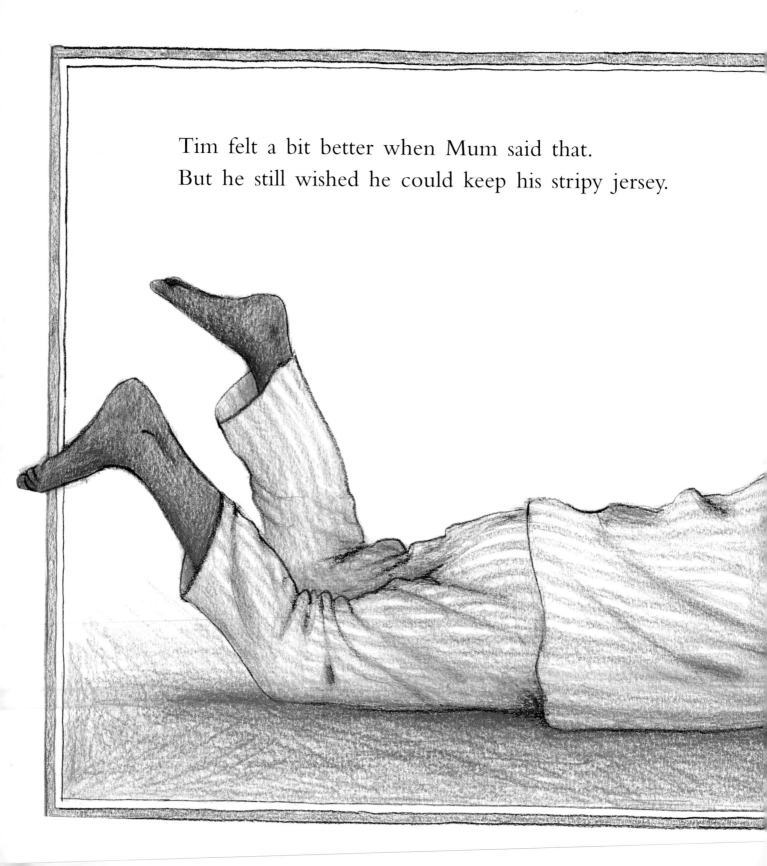

Then he looked at Toby.
"I know what we could do," Tim said.

The stripy jersey fitted Toby perfectly.
So did the Christmas-present shorts.
The teddy slippers were just right
for a bear.

Inside the give-away bag,
Mum found one of Tim's
old baby hats for Toby's head.

"You look cool, Toby," said Tim.

"He's the best-dressed bear, ever,"
said Mum. "I think we'll let him
keep those clothes."

"Okay," smiled Tim.
"But just until he gets too big for them!"